Chontae Loch Garman

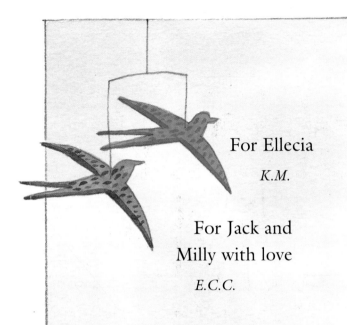

For Ellecia
K.M.

For Jack and
Milly with love
E.C.C.

First published 1994 by Walker Books Ltd
87 Vauxhall Walk, London SE11 5HJ

10 9 8 7 6 5 4 3 2 1

Text © 1994 Kate McMullan
Illustrations © 1994 Emma Chichester Clark

This book has been typeset in Galliard.

Printed in Hong Kong

British Library Cataloguing in Publication Data
A catalogue record for this book is available
from the British Library.

ISBN 0-7445-3250-7

Good Night, Stella

written by

Kate McMullan

illustrated by

Emma Chichester Clark

WALKER BOOKS
LONDON

"Good night, sleep tight,"
said Stella's father.
"Where are you going to be?"
said Stella.
"In the sitting room."
"Doing what?"
"Reading," her father said.
"Sweet dreams."

Stella's hamster galloped
on his squeaky wheel.
"Sweet dreams, Cheeko,"
whispered Stella.
Cheeko raced on.

"Dad?" called Stella.
"Why does Mum like
going to the cinema?"
"She just does," said her
father. "Good night, Stella."

Stella did not like
big dark cinemas.
And she hated scary films.
She'd seen one once
about a vampire bat.
The bat bit a woman
and left two little holes
in her neck.

Stella checked her own
neck very carefully
for fang marks.

Stella sipped
her water
and wondered
about that
woman with
the vampire bite.

When she drank,
did water spurt
out of her neck
in tiny twin
fountains?

Stella squirted
water out from
between her teeth.

Then, very quietly,
she practised gargling.

"Dad?" called Stella.
"I can't go to sleep."
"Close your eyes,"
her father said.
"You'll go to sleep."

Stella closed her eyes.

She felt her thin eyelid skin
stretching over her eyeballs.

Her eyeballs felt big. Too big.

"Dad?" called Stella.

"Can your eyeballs fall out?"

"Your *what*?"

"*Eyeballs!*"

"No," her father called back.

"They can't."

Stella lay very still.

She swallowed.

And swallowed again.

Each time she swallowed,
her Adam's apple bobbed up
and then down in her throat.

It felt like an eyeball.

Stella's father came to the door of
her room and switched on the light.
"You're a night owl tonight,"
he said, yawning. "Tell you what,
I promised your mother I'd wait up
for her, but I'm getting sleepy."

"I'll wait up!" said Stella.

"She won't be back for two hours," said her father.

"No problem," said Stella.

"OK," her father said.

"But don't go to sleep."

Stella hopped out of bed.

She put on her dressing-up hat,

flung her boa round her shoulders,

and stepped into her mother's old high heels.

"Come on, King," she said to her stuffed gorilla.

"We're off to the ball!"

Stella and King waltzed
round the room.

"Marvellous ball, isn't it?"
murmured Stella.
King just kept dancing.

"I understand it's
called the *Eye Ball*!"
King didn't say a word.

Stella picked up Melissa. She pulled off her nightie
and began putting on her lacy dress and party shoes.
"We're going out to a film," Stella told her.

"What?" said Stella. "You don't like dark, scary cinemas?"

Melissa didn't answer.

"Oh, don't be such a baby," Stella said.

Stella lined her teddy bears up at the foot of her bed.
"Once upon a time," she said, "there was a bad bat
who nibbled the fur off teddy bears' necks."

"Don't cry, bears," said Stella. "It's only a story.
Tell you what, calm down and I'll snuggle with you
under the covers."

Stella watched Cheeko zoom round and round and round. She wondered if he liked staying up all night.

If he ever felt sleepy.

If he ever closed his eyes. Just for a minute.

Cheeko's wheel squeaked on … and on … and on.

Stella's father tiptoed
into her room.
"I can't go to sleep,"
he whispered.
Stella didn't answer.
"Why don't I go
ahead and wait up
for your mother?"
Stella didn't say a word.

Her father turned out
the light and bent down
to kiss her cheek.
"Good night, Stella."